PRAISE FOR *L'AIR DU TEMPS* (1985)

"It's 1985, the MTV flag is on the moon, and Lincoln Continentals are triplicating in the New England suburb of Maple Bay, where everyone who's not in jail or divorce court is going off the deep end. A vintage murder-mystery that's evergreen as a chemically treated lawn, this smart, tight novella is the arresting and singular cry of thirteen-year-old Zinnia Zompa, who's troubling the shadows, swerving toward an awakening that might or might not be her ticket out of town."

—Kirstin Allio, author of *Buddhism for Western Children*, winner of the Iowa Review Prize for Fiction

"*L'Air du Temps (1985)* is a gorgeously written exploration of memory and childhood—of the things we choose not to know, and how they live in us against our will. Josefowicz takes us on an intoxicating deep dive into the psyche of America just before now, when consumerism was in full swing and mystery seemed to have been killed off forever. In Josefowicz's fictional Maple

Bay, mystery is far from dead—it's alive, kicking, and doing big mischief. This supremely supple, surprising, and sneaky-clever book made me start reading again the moment I finished."

—Robin McLean, author of *Pity the Beast*

"*L'Air du Temps (1985)* is a marvel, a genre-defying hybrid, a comic portrait of a 1980s New England family that's also a murder mystery. Zinnia Zompa is a fabulously astute witness to the undercurrents of her parents' unraveling marriage, all the while navigating her own shifting desires. In this gorgeous story, Josefowicz combines subtle social commentary with a radical new twist on the coming-of-age tale."

—Susan Daitch, author of *Siege of Comedians*

"Josefowicz brilliantly spins a web of desire and deception in this sly coming-of-age story wrapped around a murder mystery. At once haunting and tender, *L'Air du Temps (1985)* captures the essence of an era."

—Dawn Raffel, author of *Boundless as the Sky*

"Atmospheric and affecting, darkly funny and nostalgic, *L'Air du Temps (1985)* opens up the technicolor world of Zinnia Zompa, aged thirteen. Josefowicz has mastered the nuances of familial experience: No one is who they seem, and yet, they are exactly as they seem. The brilliance of Josefowicz's storytelling is in what she withholds, deftly showing through powerful omission all that Zinnia cannot. Visceral, restrained, intentional, and complex, *L'Air du Temps (1985)* is a transporting portrait of growing up in a family with secrets."

—Kalani Pickhart, author of *I Will Die in a Foreign Land*

"This sly novella will take you on an unforgettable ride. At first, all you'll feel is the wind blowing in through the moonroof, but beware: there's something hiding in the trunk. Josefowicz deftly steers us through beautiful, manicured suburbia, revealing the brutality just beneath the surface. A remarkable read."

—Alena Graedon, author of *The Word Exchange*

"When the murder of a neighbor jolts Zinnia Zompa's world—1980s suburban New England, complete with macrame plant slings, Sweet Valley High books, and Lincoln Continentals—the young teen is thrust toward a dawning awareness of the high, and often harrowing, cost of the American Dream. Propulsive and transporting, Diane Josefowicz's *L'Air du Temps (1985)* is filled with the shadows we pretend not to see."

—Jen Fawkes, author *Tales the Devil Told Me*

"At once nostalgic, mysterious, heart-rending, and sweet, this book is as fine and lovely as a butterfly's wing but somehow carries the weight of a entire family. Point of fact: Josefowicz has created a miracle."

—C.B. Bernard, author of *Small Animals Caught In Traps* and *Ordinary Bear*

L'Air du Temps (1985)

Diane Josefowicz

Regal House Publishing

Published by

Regal House Publishing, LLC
Raleigh, NC 27605
All rights reserved

ISBN -13 (paperback): 9781646034215
ISBN -13 (epub): 9781646034222
Library of Congress Control Number: 2023934862

Cover images and design by © C. B. Royal

Regal House Publishing, LLC
https://regalhousepublishing.com

The following is a work of fiction created by the author. All names,
individuals, characters, places, items, brands, events, etc. were either
the product of the author or were used fictitiously. Any name, place,
event, person, brand, or item, current or past, is entirely coincidental.

Printed in the United States of America

In memoriam E.C.F.G.

What stays with you latest and deepest?
of curious panics,
Of hard-fought engagements or sieges tremendous
what deepest remains?

—Walt Whitman, "The Wound-Dresser" (1865)

1

When the cops found Mr. Marfeo, he was bleeding out on the back seat of a yellow Mercury parked behind a windbreak down the airport road. From the way the blood was gushing they reckoned they'd just missed the perp, a point that came up more than once in testimony heard later by the court.

This happened in 1985, the year I turned thirteen. Mr. Marfeo was my father's accountant. He was also our neighbor in Maple Bay, where we lived in an L-shaped ranch house surrounded by lawn and shaded by a large pine tree, with a fenced run behind the garage for our dog, a smallish hound called Bixby. As soon as we moved in, my father devoted himself to landscaping, densifying the greenery with rakes and hoes and gallons of Miracle-Gro applied in manic gardening sessions after dark. He was proud of the yard, which always looked both neat and lush, and I was proud of him, in the way of children to whom parents seem as gods.

The grass was thriving. The shrubs were thriving. We seemed to be thriving too. Point of fact: we were not thriving—and later, after I learned more about the hit on Mr. Marfeo, I began to understand why.

By this time our family had reached its essential configuration—my mother and father, my kid sister, me, and Bixby. I say kid sister because back then, I had an investment in positioning. Maybe I still do. Point of fact: Zenobia was not so little. Less than a year separates our birthdays. But a lot can happen in less than a year, and something about our status as close-in-age siblings was always shadowy, not quite legit. My mother maintained that Zenobia was an accident, that she hadn't meant to fall pregnant again so soon; but then women of my mother's generation often planned their children close together to minimize "the diapers," a euphemism for time spent managing poorly contained human shit.

She did resent diapers, my mother. She liked to bully me with this reminder: *I changed your diapers.* Toward the end of her life, when diapers once again became a fact of it, it occurred to me that you might forgive a small child for shitting in a diaper. Unless I am mistaken, this is what children are like. What diapers are for. Is that not the general task of motherhood—containment? Think of the egg in its shell, or the brain in its case. Some days we were busting out. Others we could not break through fast enough.

2

As for the shooting: Maple Bay was not dangerous, but in the years after the war—the one we lost, I mean— haunt-eyed men in olive-drab fatigues drifted through the town center, giving the place an edge. They cat-called my mother as she shopped, flicking their spent cigarettes onto the sidewalk. A neighborhood associa-tion soon formed, and my father offered to lead a block watch, but the initiative foundered when my mother, who was not especially bothered by the litter or the cat-calling, joined the block walkers in a hot pink cocktail dress, causing my father to complain: *I don't understand why you have to go and make a mockery of it all, Pauline.*

Which is not to say that Maple Bay's homeowners did not have problems. They did. But their problems were different, arising from their collective talent at turning a blind eye to just about everything except the value of whatever they owned and believed they could control—their houses, their cars, the impressions they made on others. The hit on Mr. Marfeo happened right under their increasingly straight and uniform noses.

Mr. Marfeo's particular problem was a man named

James Thomson—JT, as he was known. To some, anyway. Point of fact: The name was one of several aliases. He had a wallet full of fake driver's licenses, a volatile temper, and a shock of phosphor-white hair which he slicked into a pompadour that curled slightly at the top. A man like a lit match.

JT maintained that the hair was genetic. All the men in his family had it—it was practically an heirloom.

A hair loom! Zenobia shouts across the years. *Get it, Zinn? A hair loom!*

JT met Mr. Marfeo through my father, who had hired JT as a foreman at Impeccable Pearl. My grandfather—an immigrant with an old-country name so forbiddingly consonantal that everyone just called him Skeets—had opened the factory in the 1950s, and over time he transformed a modest button shop into a leading regional supplier of plastic beads to manufacturers of costume jewelry, a booming industry in those days.

The summer before Mr. Marfeo bought it, my father hired me to work part-time in the factory office. I arrived with my father at eight on the dot, poured myself a coffee, and released the prior day's mail from its envelopes. At nine, the phone began to ring, and I spent the remainder of the day routing calls around the building. Once a week, Mr. Marfeo met with my father in the back office, which I wasn't permitted to enter. As soon as the door shut, the mood on the shop floor lightened. The ten o'clock coffee break stretched for twenty minutes, twenty-one, twenty-two.

What I'm saying is, I had reason to believe they were friends, or at least friendly. As it turned out, one aspect of their friendship involved recommending other friends for jobs, which is just what Mr. Marfeo eventually did for JT.

JT had an allure which he heightened, carefully, drawing on some inner reserve. It helped that he came from someplace else, a place where stories spoke for a man. He did like to tell them, spinning them out in his shambling drawl while the rest of the crew smoked on the loading dock and I swept the entryway free of broken glass and litter, trying to ignore the feeling of their eyes upon me, the sun hot on my back.

In my memory, JT is always sidling past me into the building's dark interior, and his jaw is always working, a story shooting out of him like a dark stream of spit from a mouthful of chaw. The door to the back office is always shut, and my father is behind it, taking calls, making plans.

3

At the trial, the cop couldn't stop talking about the mess he'd found in the Mercury: *You never saw so much blood in your life.* But JT maintained that he had seen no blood at all, not having been at the scene of the crime in the first place.

It was a crazy defense, hardly a defense at all, but JT had witnesses to back him up, people who swore that they had spent the day—a clear, blue September day—with him at a speakeasy on the other side of town.

Among those witnesses was JT's twin brother, Gary. The two were indistinguishable, right down to that wild white hair. Not even the cop who had been tailing them could say, definitively, who was who—a confusion that had its advantages, as confusions do.

Why was a cop following them? Might as well ask the wind. JT had a rap sheet as long as his drawl and twice as shambolic. Of course, he kept that part of himself turned down low. I'm sure my father had no idea, at least at first. He wouldn't have hired him otherwise. And Mr. Marfeo? I don't know what he knew.

The day of the murder, the Thomson brothers were

observed going in and out of their houses, the speakeasy, and several cars. They went in and out of one car
in particular, a silver-colored 1976 Lincoln Continental
with something interesting in the trunk. The undercov-
er cop had seen Mr. Marfeo and JT—well, someone
whose description corresponded to JT's—peering into
it.

Now, JT owned a silver Lincoln of just that make
and vintage. But so did Mr. Marfeo. Since the cop
swore the car in question had belonged to Mr. Marfeo,
it was impounded as evidence—only to be thrown out
later, when it was determined that it was the trunk of
JT's silver Lincoln, not Mr. Marfeo's, that they were
looking into.

But no one found anything in JT's Lincoln either.
Certainly nothing to prove that Mr. Marfeo had ever
been inside it. They didn't look for evidence of JT's
presence—and why would they, since it was his car?

When you assume, Mr. Kresge, my seventh-grade science teacher, liked to say, *you make an ass out of you and
me.*

A home truth, for sure. Mr. Kresge dispensed a lot
of those.

In the end, the jury found the brothers each guilty
of different things, and for his sins—or maybe I should

say his supposed sins, since at least one person, my father, persistently maintained his innocence—JT got life without parole.

Gary's out now, after twenty years. As for me, I'm thirty-five, and sick with memory.

4

Skeets opened Impeccable Pearl the same year he got married, after noticing that his bride and her friends were great consumers of cheap bead necklaces worn for a season and cast aside, only to be purchased again in different colors, as styles and seasons changed. The demand was self-renewing, the business case bullet-proof. Skeets set up shop in Honeyville, just north of Maple Bay, on the far western edge of Providence.

Oh, Honeyville, my mother liked to sigh, flashing her wild smile. *My old stomping grounds.*

She loved Honeyville, of course she did. After all, she'd grown up there. But I never understood the appeal. As far as I could tell, it was just another seen-better-days place where sag-roofed triple-deckers listed, unsteady on their pins, between low brick buildings punctuated by broken windows; a town that swung loose-hipped from the capitol like an easy girl off the arm of that night's wiseguy.

Impeccable Pearl occupied the middle floor of one of those loosey-goosey gap-toothed buildings, a small one in good-enough repair. Screwed directly into the bricks was an old-fashioned sign, hand-lettered by Skeets, that declared the company's existence.

Having bought the building, Skeets filled it with machines.

Thump: A metal wire is trimmed to one-half inch. What is called a *post*.

Thump: The post is pounded into an enameled plastic ball. What is called an *earring*.

By the gross. My father taught me that expression. Point of fact: A gross is twelve dozen, a dozen dozen, one hundred forty-four.

Point of fact: Mr. Marfeo took a total of nine bullets, three to the body, six to the face.

Who counts, counts. Something else I learned from my father.

5

Different as the two places were, Honeyville had its hooks deep in Maple Bay. I suppose my mother counted as one of those hooks, a homegirl-made-good, tastefully dressed and perfumed, *not a hair out of place*, as she liked to say. Maple Bay reeked of the same bounded sumptuousness, of freshly clipped grass and mulched flower beds. That's what people paid for, what they wanted for themselves. But the price for that fragrant order was Honeyville, which stank of grease and solvent and the fried onions that slipped from the steak-and-cheese grinders my father ate for lunch.

Don't get me wrong. I'm not judging. I'm only pointing out a relationship.

There were others. For instance, you could find Impeccable Pearl's products in the shops at Maple Bay. But you could also fail to find them.

My father liked to look, liked to find. He could make something of that. But he also liked to fail to find. He could make something of that too.

You play both sides, you can't lose—that was another of his lessons.

A scene I can't forget: He stands beside my mother at the jewelry counter of a department store. She is excited, even though her enthusiasm always prompts his irritation.

Leaning over the vitrine, she gasps: *Oh, Stanley!*

He snarls: Why buy what you can get for nothing, Pauline?

They're not the same, she says.

He cocks an eyebrow. The future flashes across his face like the shadow of an airplane where it should not be, racing along the wall of some high room.

There is something he knows that she doesn't.

He asks: My fake beads aren't good enough for you, Pauline?

They're not the same, Stanley. And you know it.

6

For a long time Skeets had needed a pacemaker. After he passed out reaching for something on a high shelf, the surgery could no longer be delayed. On the day of the operation, my father came home early, weeded the beds, and cleaned out the garage. At dusk he hung up his hoe and his rake, twisted the soapy water out of his cleaning rags, and took up a position in the kitchen, pacing back and forth beside the phone.

The call came around nine o'clock: Skeets had made it.

I took a licking and kept on ticking, he chuckled drowsily into the phone.

My mother scraped our uneaten dinners into Bixby's bowl, wiped down the tabletop, and ran a bath.

It was around this time that Skeets, deciding that he'd had enough of business, lit out for the golf course, leaving my father in charge of the factory. During this period of increased responsibility, my father trained JT in the ways of the business, ordering supplies and shipping finished product and keeping track of it all according to a system of codes recorded in a large leather ledger book. Eventually, JT had so fully absorbed the factory's day-to-day workings that my father simply could not do without him.

The discovery came as a shock. Somehow, without his knowledge or permission, my father had become dependent on a separate person over whom he did not have complete control, the very definition of an intolerable situation as far as my father was concerned. He began to scrutinize JT's behavior—his arrivals, departures, and, especially, his requests for time off from work. When JT caught the flu, his absence put my father into a weeklong funk.

At first, he tried to reason the problem away. JT's indispensability was simply the natural consequence of being an employee. To be indispensable was the *best* kind of job security, and who wouldn't want that? So long as JT wanted a job, he'd stick around.

A man would do anything for that. *Am I right, Pauline?*

Every night he did this, haranguing my mother as she stood at the kitchen counter, up to her elbows in Rice-a-Roni or Shake 'N Bake. And every night she murmured reassurance, nodding agreeably at intervals. She knew her lines and didn't hesitate to deliver them. As much as she enjoyed teasing my father, she was also good like that. Reliable. Soothing, too, when she wanted to be. But she knew the truth. We all did. My father was kidding himself. And it was precisely this basic lack of conviction that prompted him endlessly to seek reassurance from my mother. He replayed the problem of JT like some umpire's questionable call captured in slow-mo and repeated over and over. He simply could not make sense of it.

My mother bore the onslaught with a grace that still astonishes me, though given what I later learned, perhaps it should not. She didn't complain, not even when my father kept her up all night talking his way through the doubts that mushroomed continually in the damp basement of his brain. Had he not *trained* JT? Devotedly, carefully? Wasn't JT therefore, in some sense, *his* creation? Everyone knows you don't double-cross your creator. Until you do. And look what happens. Et cetera.

Even then I knew something different, but I held the knowledge close. Like JT, I wasn't supposed to have views that contravened my father's. My mother held on too. Held everything—her tongue, her anxiety, my father's clammy hand as he talked through one night after another, her boredom plain as the tightening around her eyes. Of course, she mocked him, to his face and behind his back whenever she could get away with it. But there was compassion in her stance. What my father had discovered with JT was a pain she already knew too much about. Nothing's as steady, as secure as you think.

7

My father insisted that JT owed him everything, and he was never shy about issuing reminders of a debt. He maintained that my mother owed him a great deal too.

You *got* a great deal, Stanley. May I remind *you*.

You don't need to remind me, baby.

There she stands, flushed from washing up, one slim pale hand resting on one slim canted hip, a smile playing on her lips as she mulls this marital dunning notice and my father in his easy chair prepares a rejoinder that he will preface with a wink.

Not everything was bad between them. On good days, he liked her sass. On better days, that's not all he liked.

And from one point of view, my mother did, in fact, get a great deal. She didn't come from money, and here she was with a nice house on a corner lot in Maple Bay, freed from the drudgery of finding a job and keeping it, with enough cash on the weekly to run the household—*her* household—her way. Mostly.

I won't say their marriage was happy. Who can tell about these things? My mother always said you could never know anything for sure about anyone else's domestic arrangements, what goes on *behind closed doors.*

Except the children, I suppose. They always know, even if they can't say what that knowledge is. My parents were forever dropping clues—charged looks and fierce whispered exchanges, hard retorts and drawn-out sighs. Because I didn't know what to make of them, these things rattled around my mind like pebbles in a cup. Point of fact: They're still there, still rattling. My parents' marriage wasn't happy but it was stable in the way a sapling is stable. Even in a hurricane it bends.

Well, the mother bends. My mother put down roots in my father's life, and then bent and swayed as he gusted all around her, bolstered by all the nonmaterial resources she brought to the marriage—her willingness to admire, her tolerant listening, her ability to be alone, to amuse herself, to pursue her *hobbies.*

And oh, did she have hobbies. In my mind's ear I still hear my father talking of my mother's *hobbies* in the lightly condescending tone he reserved for discussions of all the parts of her life that had nothing to do with him—her small but devoted family circle, her degree in education and her desire to use it, the pothos plant she doted on, cascading from its macramé sling behind the window in the den. His tone pared the meaning from my mother's independent activities like skin from a greening apple.

God save us, he liked to say, from your mother's *hobbies.*

Before she married my father, my mother had been a schoolteacher. Her own father, an easygoing man we called Papa Frank, had encouraged this career, and she went along with it, stopping only when I arrived. She stayed home while my sister and I were small. Papa Frank helped to babysit, keeping us busy with games— solitaire at first, then cribbage and poker—through a string of sunlit days shadowed only by the growl of my father's Mercury in the driveway, announcing the changing of the guard.

Then Papa Frank was diagnosed with cancer and had to get radiation in his lungs. By the time he beat the cancer back, Zenobia and I were attending school full-time. It was at this point that filling the days became a problem for my mother.

My father did not want her to work outside the home. But to work inside the home was impossible.

I was not put on this earth, I overheard her telling Papa Frank, to *drudge* at housework.

What about painting? Painting is a nice hobby, said Papa Frank.

That was one brilliant thing about Papa Frank: He made suggestions you could accept. She assembled materials, took night classes.

Oh, she liked to say, lightly, always lightly, *I paint.* That lightness was her admission that she would stake no serious claims. *It's a nice hobby.*

Her subjects were conventional, flowers and fruit, but she had a distinctive high-contrast style, as if she saw the world as a series of bright objects set squarely against dark backgrounds. She was good with titles too. A still life of blown white roses with drooping petals like beseeching hands she called *Joan of Arc.* A bouquet of day lilies stuck out their flaming tongues at the viewer: *Bronx Cheer.* Her paintings drew you in and made you feel things. One look and you knew: this was no hobby.

8

JT's trial made headlines for weeks. At times I thought it would never end, as if the scant half-hour of violence that had shattered one jewel-blue autumn afternoon had somehow managed to darken all the clear skies that followed, world without end, amen.

Every night my mother and I watched events unfold on the evening news. Each broadcast ended with grainy footage of security guards hustling JT down the courthouse steps, his bright pompadour lighting up a dark sea of suits and fedoras.

I ask: Maybe it's Miss Clairol?

My mother replies as I expect her to: Maybe he was born with it.

I hoot, delighted, and she grins right back at me, completing a circuit that sends a jolt to the ends of my toes. She flips her yellow hair off her shoulders and it falls back with a gorgeous heaviness, as if even gravity is in on her joke. She's been Miss Clairol-ing for so long the color might as well be natural, and she doesn't care who knows.

9

One night toward the end of the trial my mother grew pensive. If JT was still in-state, she wondered, perhaps even in a jail nearby, why couldn't my father pay him a visit and talk through whatever bad feeling had arisen between them? Would that not put an end to his obsessing?

I scoffed: Talk something *through*? *Dad*?

He wasn't always like this, Zinnia.

She lifted the pothos plant from its hook and left. I listened to the faucet running in the kitchen, I watched advertisements for Lava soap and Turtle Wax. I switched off the television, and the room fell away into an ashy darkness. The night had darkened, too, but outside was different, fresher, colder. Papa Frank was gone by this time—dead, I mean—but the loss was still too new for me to make sense of. All that registered was the cold, its variousness.

What it means to be thirteen: you scoff at your brokenhearted mother, and death just feels like a change in the weather.

My mother returned and padded to the window. She

hoisted the pot onto its hook with a soft grunt, and then she was gone in the dark.

10

My father cultivated some epic hatreds, and one of them was my mother's pothos plant. It was insignificant, just a plant—yet my father's loathing has given it an aura, a shine. I didn't inherit much from my parents, but my memory is stuffed to bursting with this charged and glittering bric-a-brac. A well-cared-for houseplant in a macramé sling can still wet my eyes.

But if I'm going to inventory their hates, I must count their loves too, and chief among my father's loves was my mother's hair, which was abundant and, thanks to her talent with Miss Clairol, nearly as light as JT's.

Sometimes she brushed it over her face, making herself a dead ringer for Cousin It. Then she'd flip it all backward, tumbling a ginger-ale wave over her shoulders and down her long back. It was a feature my father could not take from her except by main strength, and he loved her hair too much for that.

The plant, though, not so much. Like my mother's hair, the plant was abundant in its growth and graceful in its relationship to gravity. Like a child, it grew pro-

digiously in ways that could be inconvenient, blocking
light, scattering dirt, and springing the occasional leak.
It also sucked my mother's attention, which my father
coveted, as we all did. There never seemed to be enough
of her to go around.

My mother kept a paperback called *The Secret Life of
Plants* on the coffee table where my father at the end
of the day liked to rest his drink. As far as I know, she
never read the book, but every now and then she'd pick
it up and shift the bookmark. No one could say she
didn't have a sense of humor. In this way my father
came into early middle age, obsessed with an employee
and hating a potted plant.

11

In Maple Bay, the kids have the run of the neighborhood. At six years old I'm already leaving the house on my own, a few dollars stashed in my pocket along with my house key. I haunt the shopping center and skulk around the playground until other kids arrive. We play tag and jacks, tug-of-war, Red Rover.

In those days, all I want in the world is a haircut like Dorothy Hamill's. So one day after school I slip out the back door and make my way to the barbershop, alternately dragging and being dragged by Bixby. When the sidewalks end, I balance on the stone curb, pretending to be a gymnast placing one foot in front of the other on the beam. Bixby trots beside me, tail waving.

The barbershop is empty. I loop the dog's leash around a pole and walk right in, setting myself up in the chair by the window where I can keep an eye on Bixby. The barber drapes a cloth around my shoulders. *What'll it be, little lady?*

Every day Dorothy Hamill skates around an oval rink on television, and every time she leaps, spinning, into the air, her wedge haircut lifts up and comes down a split-second after she does, and at just that moment the crowd erupts. She is *so cute*. School is impossible, fractions are crazy hard, but here is one question with an obvious answer. What I want is to be Dorothy, but I'll settle for her wedge.

Give me the Dorothy Hamill, I say.

The barber replies: I like the way you think.

He spins me so I can't see the mirror. I hear the shears in action, and my hair falls to the floor in piles that remind me of the pale brown needles that collect beneath our big pine tree. Something feels tragic about this, the equation of my dead hair and those dead pine needles, but I already know that I stink at equations and I can no more stop the barber than my own breath.

X over one equals X. I am one, therefore I am X. Solution: I am a shedding pine!

The idea entertains, consoles, distracts. Already I am a person consoled by distraction, a person who makes rash decisions, regrets them, and still finds ways to avoid changing course.

The barber spins me around again to face the mirror. Worst of outcomes: I look just the same, only balder. This is not what I wanted, not at all. Smiling to hide my disappointment, I pay with a clutch of soft dollar bills.

My hair will grow back. Until it does, I'll just have to make the best of it.

I run home, the wind fresh against my newly bared neck, and twirl across the lawn. Bixby trots beside me, yipping. It must be spring, for the day is still light. Zenobia stands near the front door whipping a hula hoop around her midsection. A distant rumble becomes a roar. There is the squeal of a loose fan belt, and then there is my father behind the wheel of the yellow Mercury, pulling into the driveway.

Look, Dad! A triple *lutz*!

I launch myself into a flying turn and land badly, rolling my ankle.

Triple *klutz*, more like, my sister says, catching the hoop on her hip.

My father gets out of the car and levels me a hard stare. My insides roll. I see myself as he must see me: unchanged by a dramatic decision, still myself but with less hair. An idiot.

He hustles up the walk, blowing past me as if I don't exist.

Clapping one hand over her mouth, Zenobia makes a low sound, between a laugh and a moan: Someone's in *trrrroubblllle*.

My father's silence extends over several days during

which I am very good. Each night I cut my dinner into tiny pieces that I am careful to chew thoroughly while keeping my lips firmly sealed together. I put my clothes away after I am done wearing them instead of throwing them on the floor. I empty the dishwasher. I feed Bixby without being reminded. On the third night, I find my mother at the kitchen sink, filling the tea kettle.

What is it, Zinnia?

Daddy hates me and I don't know why!

Zinnia, she says. Calm down.

Mom. *MOM*.

Zinnia, you need to calm down. The problem is your hair.

My *hair*? Since when does Daddy care about my hair?

Not to worry. It will grow back. Your father loves your hair, you know.

He loves *my hair*?

She ruffles my new bangs. I duck away, out of reach, unaccustomed to her hands on me.

Well, he doesn't love this particular style. He loves it just the way it was before you cut it. When it was more like mine.

From a matchbook by the stove she plucks a match, strikes it, and throws it into the burner beneath the tea kettle. The flame roars up with a *whoosh*. Bixby, who has been snuggled up asleep on an old sofa cushion near the heater, opens his eyes.

But I understand why you cut it. Your sister got the golden curls, and all you got was dishwater, she says.

My mother touches the heart pendant at her neck, a gift from my father, gold as her hair, the Miss Clairol shade she has somehow magicked to my sister, leaving me to inherit her natural mouse brown. The heart is real gold, a real gift from a real store, not something he found in the stockroom at Impeccable Pearl.

With all the acid I can muster, I say: You think everything good is gold, even if it's not real.

Not real good? She smiles.

Not real *gold*.

She adjusts the heat beneath the rumbling kettle and gazes out the window into the dark yard.

Nothing gold can stay, she says, but she's not talking to me. Not really.

My hair is not pretty, I sniffle. I can only land a triple-klutz!

What can I tell you, Zinnia? I don't pretend to understand him.

12

My father fought with Skeets to keep JT on the payroll. Skeets ultimately relented but not before he imposed a condition: An employee in legal jeopardy could stay on the books so long as he hadn't been convicted of a felony—but then, in the course of the trial, JT's full rap sheet was uncovered, and so JT had to go.

When the news came down, my father kicked the ottoman. Sailed it clear across the room.

Dammit! You think you know someone.

My mother snorted. In memory, in dream, she is still snorting, her hand clapped over her mouth, barely pretending to hide her amusement. *Oh, Stanley.*

Innocent until proven guilty means nothing to my father! Nothing!

My mother twisted her mouth to rein something in—laughter, it seems to me now. It must have been laughter.

Pauline, my father urged. His guilt has not been *proven!*

His prior convictions, under a different name, included a sequence of property-related crimes. JT with his pompadour had cut a hot white swath through a territory I only knew from social studies—Kansas, Oklahoma, East Texas. Mainly he was into loan-sharking, though he had also worked a profitable sideline in stealing cars.

Grand theft auto, my mother said, whistling low. Now that's no joke.

The revelations came all at once, trailing the stench of the bad money you don't throw good money after, a taint that was spreading, subtly but pervasively, so that my grandfather was starting to wonder about my father too. Point of fact: I heard him say so. One afternoon he took me out in his new sedan—for once, not a Lincoln Continental, but a fuel-efficient Japanese car of the sort that became popular in those years after the oil shock. He was refilling the gas tank when he murmured to no one in particular: *I just don't know what has happened to my son.*

13

Night after night, my father circles the facts he has about JT, trying to square them with the man he knows, or thought he knew.

Perhaps because she has grown tired of his ruminating, one night my mother skips dinner. She calls us to the table and leaves with a box of hair coloring, a new shade called *Vintage Bubbly*. She tells us: Back in ten.

It's steak night—T-bones fried dry to save on cholesterol and served with tight fists of potatoes baked in their skins. Beneath the table Bixby shifts on his haunches; I press my feet against his hard little body, tense with the effort not to whine. My sister slides her fork through a rabble of peas, now and then lifting one to her mouth. But they keep falling, so she finally drops the fork and uses her dimpled fingers.

She still has her baby fat. There's a lot that's babyish about Zenobia. She has an unfinished quality, an arrestedness.

My mother returns wearing her bathrobe and sets

the teakettle brewing on the hob. Her hair is slicked thickly back, wet with coloring agent. She sits in her chair, tucks her feet beneath her. Her chemical smell is so intense it brings on a headache like a hot iron rod thrust between my eyes. *Oof*, I say, but quietly. Scowling, my mother pushes her hands into the mess on her head, pressing it upward. She slips a plastic-lined terrycloth turban over the mass of it and feels around the edges for strays. She checks the clock. It's important to watch the time with Miss Clairol, to get that part right.

Nothing's broken, my father says—referring, as usual, to the situation with JT.

My mother opens her mouth to speak, thinks better of it. She sighs.

Sweetie, she says, it's *all* broken.

Sweetie, my father replies, mocking her. Open a goddamned window.

My mother stands and slides behind Zenobia's chair. As she leans toward the window, her breasts swing loose, and she has to hold the front of her robe closed with one hand as she reaches for the window clasp.

Let me, I say, rising. I can get it.

She steps back, adjusting her robe: Thanks, Zinnia.

Nothing's broken, my father repeats. Nothing that can't be fixed or replaced.

Stanley, my mother says. Can we talk about something else? Please?

She is using her reasonable voice, the one she uses with me whenever I dig my heels in. The night, cool and damp, seeps into the hot kitchen. Somewhere nearby a dog barks once, twice, and Bixby twitches. My father hacks at the remains of his T-bone. When he and Zenobia finish eating, they head for the den.

It's my turn to load the dishwasher. I scrape the plates into Bixby's bowl and pour in some chow. He eats greedily, tail waving. My mother regards him from her chair.

His tremor's worse, she says.

He's getting old, I reply. He's gray around the muzzle, and he wobbles if he has to stand too long.

I hadn't noticed, my mother says.

I'm loading the dishwasher, trying to maximize the useful space. In the den, the easy chair squeaks as my father reclines in it, and then there's the snap of the television coming on and the noise of canned laughter.

At the counter my mother drops an ice cube into a juice glass and adds a finger of Scotch.

Ready? she asks me.

I shrug. Sure.

Don't forget the lights, she says.

I follow her into the den where she gives the drink to my father before taking her usual place on one end of the sofa. I take mine at the other. My sister is stretched on the floor doing her Spanish homework.

Change the channel, would you, Zinnia?

But I just sat down.

You're young, my father says. You can always sit down again.

I stand up and switch the channel. He stops me after one turn.

Hold it right there, he says. Let's watch the game.

My mother sniffs.

Now, Pauline—

Can I sit down now, please?

Mi familia está loco, Zenobia murmurs. Or is it *loca?*

Her worksheet endures a bout of furious erasure.

You want some help? I ask, settling back on the sofa.

Hoy NO, grinGO.

With my toe I tap the doughy flesh of her back where it pokes out above the waistband of her pants, plaid polyester hand-me-downs that I am extremely glad to have outgrown. She finds a small hole in the rug and enlarges it with the tip of her pencil.

Stop it, I hiss. *That costs money.*

What I know about money could fit on the nub of

Zeno's eraser. I am just repeating things my father says.

And now he is saying: A man needs a second chance, Pauline.

Hush, Stanley. Let's just watch the game. I can catch *Murder, She Wrote* another time.

My father rattles the ice in his glass. She takes the empty and rises, heading for the kitchen. But at the threshold she turns around.

Surely you knew what he was.

Come again, Pauline?

Nothing. Never mind. Forget it.

My father rises from his chair and turns the television off. Glancing up at me, Zenobia sticks out her tongue, dark with graphite. Our reflections are bright in the darkened window; the memory is bright still.

Hey, says Zenobia.

Hey, I say.

But my father's already gone, lost to his private struggle. In the kitchen he's shouting: JT's brother Gary got a sentence, a shorter one—*with parole*! All JT did—all anyone could *prove* he did—was drive the Mercury!

Stanley—

He was *seen* to have been driving the Mercury. It matters who does the seeing, Pauline! How good their eyes are.

Stanley, please. Don't you think a bright yellow Mercury's kind of hard to miss?

My father makes a choked sound. Never mind, he says sourly. Leave me alone.

That night my mother goes to bed early, leaving my father to doze before the television. When he begins to snore, Zenobia puts her homework away. A faucet runs in a far part of the house.

In my parents' bedroom, the streetlight sheds its wan light over my mother's long frame. She is stretched out on top of the bedspread, the length of her covered in a white flannel nightgown.

I have her lanky build. When I look in the mirror, I don't see my mother yet, but I see less and less that reminds me of Zenobia.

Her eyes are closed.

Mom!

She raises and lowers one long, pale hand, her fingers ghost petals on the droop.

Did JT kill Mr. Marfeo?

Without lipstick, her lips are the same non-color as her skin. When she speaks they barely move: *Zinnia, please.*

Sorry, I say.

From outside comes the purr of an engine. Through

the window, I see the Mercury's taillights recede down the dark driveway.

My mother groans.

Go to bed, Zinnia. Don't make me tell you twice.

I make a last pass through the house. In the kitchen my father's rinsed glass rests overturned, drying on a tea towel. I refill the dog's water dish. I switch off the driveway lights. When I find a permission slip for an upcoming school expedition that Zenobia has neglected to tell anyone about, I sign my father's signature and tuck the slip back into her school bag, leaving it at the top where she's sure to find it. Forgery aside, I like this image of myself, a helpful person who smooths out bumps in her kid sister's day.

I return to the den and curl into the recliner. Sunk into the pit left by my father's body, I knock my chin against my kneecap, pleased by the newly risen bone. He'll be back. Or he won't. I'm waiting for something— but then what teenager isn't waiting for something?

14

Pick me, PICK ME! The classroom is roaring. We stretch after our waving hands, pressing ourselves upward like seedlings after a heavy application of Miracle-Gro. Mr. Kresge, my science teacher, has a special assignment for one of us. Just one. He will choose.

Me, me, ME!

The assignment is always the same. He has left something crucial on his car's front seat, and he needs a student to run out to the parking lot and retrieve it. It could be anything—his lesson plan, his lunch, his eyeglass case. It doesn't matter what it is. The great draw is the hall pass. You can do anything with a hall pass, go anywhere.

That day it's my turn. Mr. Kresge has forgotten his newspaper and he needs it for today's class. Point of fact: I'm not imaginative about hall passes, so I just run out to the parking lot. It's so warm the asphalt sticks to the soles of my sneakers.

Mr. Kresge drives a Mercury that's the same chrome-yellow as my father's but a slightly different make. He calls it The Big Banana. It's easy to spot.

The newspaper's folded on the dusty dash. I can see what it is he wants to teach: There's a front-page story about interferon, the miracle drug that might finally cure cancer. Maybe it's the one thing that can save Papa Frank, who has been feeling too lousy to visit, making my mother worry that his cancer has come back. I try not to think about it, but this takes a surprising amount of effort. On the way back, I hold Mr. Kresge's key wallet so tightly the pointy edges of the keys pinch my palm through the leather, which leaves behind a faint smell of Mr. Kresge's aftershave.

I don't wash my hands again that day, I just keep sniffing. Even then I must have understood, on some deep level, that our banal automotive obsessions screened others, less tame: when to leave, where to go, how to get there.

15

After many loud fights, my father permits my mother to go back to work part-time.

The timing made sense. By this point—it must have been around 1983—I was in junior high, taking the bus to and from school. Although Zenobia was still in elementary, she was big enough to walk home on her own. We could handle ourselves, my mother insisted. But in order to work, my mother needed a car—and in her need my father must have spied an opportunity.

One Saturday morning we drive to the used car dealership through a sudden rain that lashes the windshield as the wipers pound: *lub-dub, lub-dub*. By the time we arrive the rain has let up and the sun heats the air so fast we step out into a dense jungle atmosphere. Rainbows paint the greasy surfaces of every puddle. There's another oil slick on my face, heralding zits galore tomorrow.

It can't be later than ten in the morning but already the day is *diabolical*—a word I like because of one of its meanings: having two heads. So much of what's hard about life involves duplicity.

A man approaches, blown by a gust that has caught in the sail of his huge black umbrella. He shines from the roots of his Brylcreemed hair to the tips of his oxblood cordovans. He acts like he knows us, or knows someone who does.

He pumps my father's hand: Nice to see you, Mr. Zompa. How's it going, Mr. Zompa. What brings you, Mr. Zompa.

How ya doing, my father says flatly, to shut down the salesman's smarmy rat-a-tat.

Oh my! Aren't those rugrats getting big!

My father murmurs: As rugrats do.

My mother talks over him: They're in school all day, every day.

With a smile suggesting he's had this exact conversation a hundred times, the salesman says: Let me guess, Mrs. Zompa. You're looking to go back to work.

My father briefly sucks an invisible and very sour lemon. Then, seeing me, his expression changes to something blander and more benign. He launches into a story, the outlines of which might plausibly have been ours—if you didn't know us. From this story he omits important details, like the fact that the whole idea of my mother working just makes him want to spit. We are not supposed to lie to adults, or to anyone, so it is interesting to hear my father pick and choose his facts. *Diabolus*, I think. Two-faced.

So the lady's going back to work, says the salesman in his folksy way, bonhomie-ing as hard as he can. Those narrow cordovans look like they hurt.

There is no stopping her when she gets a bee in her bonnet, my father says pseudo-amiably.

My mother narrows her eyes. My father rests his palm on the small of her back, catching the ends of her hair. She does a little shimmy, freeing them, and he takes his hand away.

A gal can't spend her days on the sofa eating bon-bons, she says.

My mother never says "gal." She's lying, too, but in a different way.

You don't look like a gal who eats bonbons, says the salesman. He nods appreciatively at my father, who acknowledges this tribute with a half-smile. It's either that or slug him. The light shifts in my father's eyes as he weighs his options.

You know, I might have just the thing, says the sales-man, quickly now that he's sensed his mistake. Come on in, he says. It's like the Devil's hotbox out here.

We follow him into the showroom, a huge glass-enclosed space. The hem of my shorts lifts on a draft of cool, conditioned air. High up, a disco ball turns, sending dots of light around the room. In the center, directly beneath the disco ball, a long gray car spins on the biggest lazy Susan I have ever seen. The car looks like something between a spaceship and a limo, with porthole windows on either side of the back seat. The salesman hits a switch and the car stops spinning.

In the corner, a television shows the MTV flag, waving on a pole that has been planted on the moon.

Look! Zenobia whispers, excited.

Don't be a moron, I hiss. Everyone knows there's no wind on the moon.

She turns large full eyes on me. I've been mean, and I should know better. But now is not the time for her to start bawling. I glance at my father, but he is absorbed in conversation with the salesman.

That was a joke, Zeno! Don't be a baby.

She reddens and the tears overspill. She looks away, wipes her face on her sleeve. Don't call me a baby.

Don't be one, then.

She pouts.

That's simple logic, I tell her.

The salesman stands on the dais, teetering in those narrow shoes. My father offers him a hand, but he waves him off and rights himself in three quick steps.

Brushing his lapels, he stalks toward the passenger door, as nonchalant as a housecat who has just nearly overturned the aquarium.

The Lincoln Continental Mark IV, he intones. Twenty feet long, seven feet wide, this baby tips the scales at five thousand pounds.

My mother murmurs, That's a lot of bonbons.

Pauline, my father warns.

It's not the latest model, the salesman continues. But the odometer tells the real story. Not a hundred miles on her.

That is a wiseguy car, observes my mother.

It's not just for wiseguys, says the salesman. There's a new tightness around his mouth.

My mother seems unsure whether to scowl or grin. It's a look I recognize.

Stanley, doesn't JT have one of these?

No idea how he manages it on what I pay him, my father says.

The salesman heaves open the passenger door and shoves the front seat forward, motioning for me and Zenobia to climb into the back. To make up for being mean, I help Zenobia onto the dais and let her go first into the car. The interior is dark, and the seats are covered in maroon velour that's so dense and cool, it's like sitting in the lap of a plush toy. Everything smells like Lemon Pledge.

My mother stands beside the car and peers at us through the windows. The salesman opens the car door on the driver's side, preparing to usher my father in.

How is she on gas? my father asks.

Almost ten miles to the gallon, Mr. Zompa.

Sheesh.

Aw, Mr. Zompa. Don't tell me you ain't got the *scarole.*

He rubs his fingers together, a neighborhood gesture, as he continues: We got a grapevine in this town, and *I* know that *you* know what it takes to make your own good Chianti!

My father groans. He has gotten into economizing habits, taking his foot off the gas on the downhills to save fuel. Money's tight.

Anyway, the salesman continues, turning to my mother, with all the extra cabbage you'll be making on your new job, you can afford it.

With her fingers my mother brushes the gold heart at her neck.

The back seat is so velvety I want to stretch across it, but Zenobia is settled on the other side and she looks ready to bite my head off.

The salesman turns up the charm, pointing out features of the interior: the leather-wrapped steering wheel, the ashtray covers patterned with glossy amber swirls. That's burled wood, says the salesman. I press it, and it pops open to reveal a spotless metal declivity. Ashtray, says the salesman, as if I don't know.

My mother folds herself into the maroon depths of the passenger seat.

Comfy? the salesman asks as he shuts the door. Across the room, the glass wall rises to the ceiling like an immense garage door, opening the way to the parking lot. They're all in, Mr. Zompa. Why don't you take it for a spin?

My father relents and gets behind the wheel. The dais drops slowly until we're level with the floor and my father rolls us out as the salesman gestures directions—a little to the left, a little to the right. In the parking lot, the car starts to heat up. My father turns a knob and cool air issues from hidden vents. He takes us onto the main road, the big wheel turning easily under his hands.

So this is power steering!

My mother's seat comes toward me, making a mechanical sound. She tries different angles, tilting herself forward and backward.

Power everything, she says. No wonder Binkie Marfeo loves her husband. If only we knew what he did for a living.

Doesn't matter, says my father. He's making it.

All that rich living, my mother clucks.

My father snorts.

You'll see, Stanley. It'll come back to bite them in the end.

Approaching the highway, my father makes a big show of checking all the mirrors. There's plenty of time for this safety theater because the car is not exactly zippy. As we lumber up the on-ramp, he gooses the gas repeatedly.

Jesus, he mutters. Can't say this thing has much pep.

My mother presses a button in the ceiling. Part of the roof slides right back, so there's nothing between us and the blue sky. She whistles.

So that's how a moonroof works.

It's a sunroof, Pauline.

Moonroof, my mother insists. It's a moonroof.

A deep thrum rises from the floorboards and settles in my chest. My heart beats out of step, another engine with its own imperatives. Maybe when I am old, I will also need a pacemaker.

We finally reach my father's familiar driving speed—

altogether too fast, is how my mother describes it, though she never sounds like she's complaining. Now the ride is frictionless, like sailing—well, what I imagine sailing's like, not that I've ever actually done it. Or much else, for that matter.

These days I feel my greenness acutely. My mother says this self-consciousness is normal, it goes with the greasy face and the zits. *This too shall pass*, she tells me.

Well, what the fuck does she know?

I slide a finger across the ashtray cover and press it just to make it pop. I do this over and over, harder and faster, until my father warns: *Zinnia.*

We ride down the highway and back again, making the circle a few times. As we turn back into the dealership my father spins the wheel and brakes hard, in a way that would have produced a huge squeal if we'd been driving in his Mercury, doing a move he calls *burning rubber*. But this time nothing burns, there is no sound, just the slow skid. My father's eyes roll in their sockets, loose with some emotion; I still can't call it fear.

Even now, after so much time, I still can't call it fear.

Back in the lot, the Mercury looks as dingy as our basement's linoleum. The bright sun brings out all the pits in the windshield.

My father complains to the salesman: You know

she's kind of hard to stop once you get her started.

Well, that sounds like just your kind of thing, Mr. Zompa. What with your old lady and that bee in her bonnet.

It took a good thirty seconds to reach, ah, *cruising speed*, my father presses.

The salesman waves vaguely toward a distant part of the lot where low-slung speed-racers crouch like runners on their marks.

You want something fast, Mr. Z? I've got plenty of options for you. But with a Lincoln Continental, you don't need speed. Folks see you coming and get the hell out of your way.

16

Our lives revolved around cars—who had one, what kind, which extras they shelled out for. *Put the pedal to the metal*, our parents urged us as we dallied over some distasteful task. *Highway robbery*, we clucked, meaning something was overpriced. Smart kids were *fast-tracked* into tougher classes. When life handed you a lemon, you sold it for parts.

In junior high, I stake a claim to independence by comparing everything not to cars but to the human reproductive system. Even the new Lincoln seems like nothing so much as a giant uterus in a can.

One night my mother takes us for a drive. Zenobia calls shotgun, so I'm stuck in the back. I push my sneakers beneath the driver's seat and poke and wiggle until my mother sighs: *Zinnia.* You are poking me in the cooch.

The cooch! I shout.

My mother says, That's an in-the-car word.

We're out joyriding because there's nothing else to do after our mother silences the television with a dramatic gesture involving all the small bones of her hand. The television annoys her, but not as much as my father does when he is snoring in front of it, nearly horizontal in his recliner.

My mother takes a route I don't recognize that leads down a dark road that runs alongside the railroad tracks. Above us rise tall pine trees, shadowed black against the night's deep blue. Mom keeps her eyes on the road and her jaw clenched. This is how she drives when she knows where she wants to go but isn't exactly sure how to get there.

Salt air blows in through the moonroof.

The beach! I smell the beach!

Zenobia says, You definitely smell.

Fuck you, I tell her.

My mother, quietly: *Language,* Zinnia.

You smell *something,* Zenobia says. You didn't let me finish.

That's a big fat lie, and you're a big fat liar!

Girls, please. I'm trying to think, my mother says.

We pass a row of townhouses so new that there are still lines between the strips of sod that make up the front lawn. These buildings have been going up everywhere because all the parents in Maple Bay are getting divorced, and each freshly fractured family requires two separate houses.

Wah-lah, my mother says as we pull up to the town-house at the end of the row. Its front door is lit by a boxy lantern hanging from the underside of the porch roof.

And who do you think lives *here*?

I don't know.

Ha! You don't know. Well, I'll tell you, Zinnia. That's where Mr. Kresge lives.

He does?

How does she know this very private fact about him? How does she know *anything* about him?

Zenobia hums: *Nah nah, nah nah.*

The road ends suddenly in a cul-de-sac. In the distance is a shifting dark mass—the ocean.

What if he sees us, Mom?

My mother spins the wheel. Not to worry, she cries. We have power steering!

Oh my God, this is embarrassing. How could any-one miss our huge silver Lincoln making a K-turn in this tiny cul-de-sac?

I slide down in the seat until I'm fully horizontal and slip down further still, onto the floor.

I have my own small collection of facts about Mr. Kresge, observations I settle in the Trapper Keeper of my mind: He has an advanced degree in biology. He leaves his shirts untucked. He is tall and a little sway-backed. He wears black loafers that make his feet look like loaves.

The truth is, I have a huge crush on Mr. Kresge. And somehow, though I have said exactly nothing about it, my mother seems to know.

My mother presses the gas. The car responds slug-gishly, which is probably for the best because I'm pretty sure she isn't completely aware of where the road ends. Blood roars in my ears. From the wheel well, I pant:

Mom. *Mom*—

Oh, for God's sake. Calm down, Zinnia. I just thought you'd appreciate the view.

Back on the highway, we speed homeward down a road so deserted there are not even moths in the head-lights. It's hours past bedtime. My mother stomps on the gas pedal and the car hitches briefly before shoot-ing down the road so fast we outrun our headlights—at which point, she switches them off.

Useless, she growls.

We're flying now through the darkness. My mother's face seems like a lantern, lit from within.

17

Guinea canoe, our handyman calls our new car. Freddy Hallam has a colorful way of talking.

Freddy lives in the faraway part of the state where everyone's name ends in a consonant and every road ends across the border in Connecticut, where huge trees cast dappled shade on deep green lawns ringed by white fences and where life really must be different. Although my mother comes from Honeyville, *her people* come from this place. My father's do not, and those are the people Freddy has in mind when he talks about *guineas* and their *canoes*.

Not in my father's presence, of course. Freddy might not be educated, but he's not stupid.

In his own words: *I know which side my bread's buttered on.*

My mother says we have to be patient with Freddy. She refers to something called *noblesse*, something else called *ooo-bleege*. She means we have to put up with him. We may not be wealthy like the Marfeos—who have a swimming pool they pay good money to maintain all summer long, even while they are away on vacations in

Europe—but we still have Freddy. More precisely: In lieu of swimming pools and fancy trips, my mother has Freddy, and she intends to keep him.

When Freddy comes, she doesn't go to work. She stays home and runs errands to make his day go easier. If he needs a bag of nails, she drives to the hardware store. If he needs a hammer, she does just the same. This way he doesn't have to stop working.

But stopping work is not Freddy's problem. His trouble is getting started.

He usually spends his first hour on the job sitting at our kitchen table. My mother fixes coffee, and they talk as he drinks cup after cup. She sets out Stella D'oro cookies, an elegant plate of golden-baked G-clefs. He smokes one cigarette and then another. Gearing up, he calls it. While he enjoys these refreshments, she stands before her easel and paints.

Home from school with a sore throat, I sit in a patch of sunlight nibbling toast while my mother fixes coffee for Freddy. Freddy leans way back in his chair and cocks his thumbs under his suspenders as he goes rattling on about my mother's favorite topic, Mrs. Marfeo. Who aggravates my mother fiercely, especially when she passes our house behind the wheel of her Lincoln Continental, which is just like ours.

Mom doesn't like the duplication. She forgets that it is we who are the real copycats. We got our Lincoln after the Marfeos got theirs.

It's better not to point out these facts, as my mother finds them *inconvenient*, and inconvenience is not *conducive to her peace*. But it's true: Binkie Marfeo was driving that car long before my father bought one of the same make and model for my mother.

The car rolls past, slowly. I can see it through the picture window.

Look at her out there, Freddy says. His eyebrows go up and down, an invitation.

My mother frowns. *Again?*

I don't know why Mom gets so upset. Binkie lives down the street. Of course she drives past our house ten times a day. And it's not like Binkie had been so original in her choice of auto. Even JT has a Lincoln, and that's probably why my father wanted one. JT must have given him the idea.

Oh yeah, she's out there every three minutes in her guinea canoe.

Little pitchers, my mother warns him, cocking a thumb in my direction.

Won't do her any harm. That guinea canoe is just like yours, Pauline!

Freddy, please stop with this business about a *guinea canoe.*

I blush hot and hard. *Guinea* is an inside-the-house word, not a word for company. Why not? I don't know, and I am afraid it's because the word is somehow related to the human reproductive system. But the only guinea I have ever heard of is a pig. Maybe it's a metaphor. My father says there are *guineas* all over Hollywood, and even I know the place is filled with pigs. But a *guinea* might also be money. At the library, a book called *Three Guineas* stands out, eye-level on the shelf. I haven't read it, but on the cover is an illustration of loose change. It's next to a book called *Sartor Restart Us*, which I don't even need to take off the shelf to know it's going to bore me. The misspelling on the spine is plain stupid, and ever since our trip to the automotive showroom I can't abide anything having to do with cars.

What's with all the ducats? I asked Freddy once, when he was talking about *guineas.*

The Duckettes? Are they on MTV? He paused. Don't say *guineas*, kid. It's rude.

Now Freddy shakes the contents of a pink packet into his coffee.

Got any cream, Pauline?

But there is no cream. Ever since Skeets developed his heart condition, my mother has been afraid my father will go the same way—first the pacemaker, then the golf course, then something else. The grave, I guess. So she put our family on a diet. No more sugar and cream for us; she replaces all the good stuff with what she calls *skinny substitutions*—pink packets of fake sweetener, blue gallons of skim milk. Instead of pats of Land-o-Lakes, I spread my toast with globs of I Can't Believe It's Not Butter. When I finish, I play with the lid, moving it up and down like a mouth, the way it moves on the commercial, saying: *Butter. Butter. Butter.*

You gone deaf all of a sudden, Pauline? This coffee could use a splash of cream.

I cry out: *Parkay-ay!*

Zinnia! Stop that noise this instant and get the cream for Freddy.

She waves toward the fridge with a paintbrush loaded with pink paint. Today she is painting a portrait of Freddy, whose face in the hot kitchen has indeed gone very pink.

But there is no cream!

You heard me.

I scramble to my feet and retrieve a jug of bluish skim milk from the fridge. As I set it on the table, Freddy waggles his thick gray eyebrows.

You call this cream, Pauline?

It's better for you, Freddy. You have to take care of your heart.

Is that so?

He lights another cigarette.

My mother shrugs, smearing Freddy-colored tones onto her palette. She's not a *guinea* so she doesn't worry about getting fat. The rest of us though, are fatties. Pigs.

I slither down to the floor and turn back to my reading, a Sweet Valley High novel that I found in Zenobia's room. All these books are boring. In this one, the class clown trains for a pizza-eating contest, and already I know how the book will end. No self-respecting *guinea* would have to train for that.

You know, Freddy, my father even put a red bow on the radiator.

Zinnia, my mother warns. Let's not tell tales.

After our trip to the dealership, where no deal was concluded as far as I could see, the car just turned up in the driveway. No bow, no nothing. Of course I'm telling tales. Someone has to fill in the blanks.

Freddy stubs out his cigarette. My mother frowns and clucks to still him; it's hard to capture a subject in motion.

Quite an imagination on this rugrat, he says. So, Zinnia, what's next? You gonna tell me you still believe in Santy Claws?

18

Occasionally we were capable of acting like a normal family. My parents were in some ways exactly like other parents I knew, bubbling over with private grown-up jokes and sly winks, house-proud and generally worried about money. My father fretted about our new home's mechanicals and saved to install central air; my mother fretted about the azaleas and the rhododendrons; they both fretted about the price of gas. Above all, they loved their circular driveway and their wide garage, space for the cars they intended to own and to display. But the only times I ever saw them really happy were on vacations. They loved each other only when they were away from the home they were making together. Or maybe what they loved was being on the road.

The summer after the arrival of the Lincoln, they planned a cross-country trip. I imagined two weeks of lounging on the velour back seat with the AC cranked, listening to the radio while gliding through unending cornfields and grassland prairies pocked with buffalo hollows, divots filled with purple flowers like in *Little House on the Prairie.*

Before we left, Papa Frank promised to look after the dog, and he gave me and Zenobia a huge bag of butterscotch candies. *For the road*, he said.

On family trips the routine is always the same. Up early to match the pace of my father's sleep cycle; he is a depressive early riser. Stacks of pancakes for breakfast, a box of donuts for the road. A long morning ride that ends when the day's heat overcomes the AC. If there's an attraction—a petting zoo, a scenic overlook—we might stop and take its measure. If we're hungry, we load up on apples and oranges, or a box of ice-cream bars if my father feels indulgent. After that, my mother opens our Triple-A guide and reads us the listings. Two stars is my father's limit; anything more, he says, is a tourist trap. My mother has other requirements. She won't stay anywhere that doesn't have a steakhouse for my father and a heated swimming pool for me and Zenobia.

But, Mom, I say, what do *you* want?

She wiggles her toes in her sandals, which are made of cork and rise up six inches. She smiles at my father, a smile that takes us all in. Her sunglasses are red and heart-shaped.

She says: I don't need much. *A loaf of bread, a jug of wine, and thou.*

Okay, I say, receding hot-faced into the back seat.

My mother slides across the front seat and my father puts his arm around her. He slips downward, so she can rest her head on his chest.

The butterscotch candies last through Pennsylvania. Zenobia doesn't like them, but I am addicted; no sooner does one dissolve in my mouth than the next softens in my palm. Sometimes our luggage shifts, a soft *chunk*, in the trunk, but the ride is otherwise quiet, sunlit, butterscotched.

An itch—a black ant, crawling up my leg.

Dad! Ants!

The car, my God—the car is *full* of ants. I slap frantically, wanting to get them away but also hoping one will land on Zenobia.

Aggh, get it off!

My father throws a hard glance over his shoulder. Told you that would happen, he says. And did you listen? You did not.

Someone—I have my suspicions as to *who*—has pushed a dozen or so half-sucked butterscotch candies into the gap between the rear seat and its housing. Now the ants have moved in, and there is no evicting them without taking the whole car apart.

They are most active in the early part of the day. Zenobia and I spear them with plastic cocktail toothpicks, the kind that are injection-molded into pirate swords and hold the fruit that comes with our Shirley Temples, and scrape them against the edges of the open windows. One by one, dead ants whirl into the fumes of our car exhaust. We are scattering dead ants across the continental United States, from the mountains to the prairies to the oceans white with foam! And if those prairies are dotted with divots full of purple flowers, I wouldn't know, because I do not see them. I see only ants.

Dead ant, *dead ant*, my sister sings. Dead ant, dead ant, dead ant, dead ant, dead *annnnnnnt*—

Nearing California, my father jabs his finger toward a distant pumpjack well.

That's what they call a nodding donkey, he says.

It doesn't look like a donkey to me. It does nod, however—they all nod, like metronomes, rising and falling, slow, slow, slow. But then nothing moves fast in the heavy desert air, certainly not a huge silver car containing a family of tourists and their luggage and their ants.

Maybe it's the bad air, or the hypnosis of the road, but I fall into a daze, lulled by the desert and the state of mind it evokes in my parents. Previewing the rest of the trip, they intone the names of famous places we'll visit—Big Sur, Mount Tam—and discuss important landmarks, bridges, and canals. They sound as if they know the place, as if California might be just the westernmost outpost of Maple Bay. It isn't, but I have trouble believing this until we reach Los Angeles, where the skyscrapers are taller than any I have ever seen, narrow rivers of dark glass that run straight up into the sky, edged with something golden brown called *smog*—another new piece of vocabulary.

We glimpse the HOLLYWOOD sign and the air inside the car becomes electric. My father stops to gas up the car and disappears into a plexiglass-fronted hut, looking to pay the cashier. He returns with a box of donuts and a six-pack. On the highway again, my parents chatter excitedly, talking over each other as if we can't hear, about the films they might watch later, after we go to sleep. *Hair. Silkwood.* A sexist movie called *10,* which my mother tolerates because my father insists she is a dead ringer for the star, a mostly naked Bo Derek.

He pulls a donut from the box and offers it to my mother.

No thanks, she says. I've had too many donuts.

Nonsense, Pauline. You can never have too many donuts.

Oh, contraire! What you can never be, Stanley, is too thin or too rich.

My father sighs: To be and to have.

My mother sighs: To have and to hold.

She reaches out to brush a smudge of powdered sugar from his cheek. When she's done she sucks her fingers. We speed past two women hitchhiking. They're young, blond, attractive. One wears bellbottoms and a porkpie hat, too warm for the desert. The other's in a miniskirt, no shoes, bare midriff.

That girl has never seen a donut in her life, my mother says.

My father says nothing, keeps his eyes on the road.

Bo Derek, she continues sourly, does not eat donuts.

For God's sake, Pauline, all I did was offer you a donut.

She hands my father a can of beer, saying: For your sins.

He sets it between his legs and curls back the tab. My mother presses a button and the moonroof slides open with a greased whir. In the distance, a nodding donkey rises and falls along with my mother's chest beneath her favorite T-shirt, a thin red one that asserts "Je t'aime" in flowing white letters. She flips down the visor and finds her image in the mirror. She coats her lips with a pale lipstick named "Desert Sand."

We are speeding, burning time, petroleum derivatives, our unplentiful dollars. I still remember the dryness of the desert, how the roof of my mouth longed for my tongue, how the roof of the sky longed for something else. What would you long for, if you were the sky? An airplane—or the earth, so distant, so not in need of you?

Stop kicking, my mother warns. I don't want to feel your feet.

Now you can smell them, says Zenobia, lifting her legs over the front seat to wiggle her bare toes into the space between Mom and Dad.

Laughing, my mother bats Zenobia's feet away. After glancing at us in the rearview mirror, my father tips the can to his mouth and swallows noisily. He drinks for a long time, lubricating himself for something, perhaps another lecture, one of his thoughts gone so long and curdled it has to be shared or else he will explode.

He drains the can and flings the empty out the window. It caroms against a highway sign, the one that keeps coming up like a card I can't stop picking—California 1, the green of spades. I still recall the capacity of the gas tank: twenty-three gallons.

We're playing our one cassette, a special compilation that came with the car. My mother punches the buttons to make her favorite song repeat but the tape's wearing out, and the words are hard to hear. I get a John Denver brain worm anyway: *Take me home, bumpy roads.* The brain worm stays loud in my mind all afternoon, even as I'm sinking down into the motel pool's depths, and only stops when, touching bottom, I jerk my foot back from the sucking drain, surprised by its urgency, the way it seems to want me closer.

19

The summer ends but school does not begin, leaving all of us at loose ends. The teachers have gone on strike, and my mother, who is not union—she would need a full-time position for that—is home as well, showing something she calls *solidarity*, a word I only know from newscasts featuring a man named Lech Walesa who is always raising his fist and shouting about working conditions at some shipyard in Poland. I'm tired of being home all day with my mother, and I don't care about solidarity or shipbuilders or Poland, so after two days my father takes me to work with him. That morning JT shows up at the factory and punches in as if he never left. As soon as he sees me, he gives a low whistle.

Looking good, Zinnia, he says.

He's leaning on the Dutch door that separates the lobby from the front office. I'm wearing a short skirt that shows off what's left of my California tan, and his compliment makes me blush from my groin to the roots of my hair.

Cat got your tongue, honey?

Thank God for the phone, which is ringing. Dry-mouthed, I lift the receiver: Good morning, Impeccable Pearl.

JT sidles away, onto the factory floor, and I am relieved not to see him again that day. Mom picks me up at three and returns me to the cool sanctuary of the house. I gulp down a can of Diet Coke and wander outside barefoot, enjoying the feel of the grass beneath the soles of my feet.

That night my father comes home breathless.

Pauline! JT is back!

Oh, Stanley. Why?

My father doesn't know. He pressed JT for details, but JT just said that he had excellent reasons for being parsimonious with explanations.

I hope he's learned something from his time in the pokey, my mother said.

Innocent until proven guilty, Pauline. May I remind you.

He's out on bail, may I remind *you*.

He wants to settle down. Wants to find a wife, buy a house. It's very natural. A man needs to settle down eventually. He's at that stage.

What he needs is to demonstrate that he's not a flight risk. When does his trial begin?

You don't understand, Pauline.

Maybe I do, and maybe I don't.

With JT's return my father cheered up, but toward my mother he stayed cool. He restricted her weekly allowance, telling her she could make up the difference herself as soon as the strike ended and she went back to work.

But I need things to teach, Stanley. Proper clothes. The kids don't have pencils. I have expenses.

Expenses, he says nastily. I'll *bet* you have expenses.

That night the phone rings long and loud enough to wake me. I roll over, cooling my hot ear against the wall, through which I hear my father say: *JT, I have an idea.*

20

One day the Lincoln showed up in the driveway. Another day it disappeared. Easy come, easy go. Now you see it, now you don't. These phrases described the facts but could not explain them.

By this time I was in eighth grade. School had finally started after a week of last-ditch negotiations between the city and the teachers' union. I had Mr. Kresge again for science, and I'd gone out for cross-country, which he coached. That afternoon Mom was picking me up from practice. The day had been rainy and I'd caught a chill. When she found me in the lobby, I was covered in goose bumps and my stomach growled so loud and long her eyes briefly saucered.

Let's get you home, Zinnia. You need a hot shower and something to eat.

Out in the parking lot it's almost dark. Headlights are bearing down on us from the main road. My mother stares at the spot where she swears she has just parked the car. She looks to the sky: Oh, Christ. *Christ.*

I shiver. My damp running clothes are totally insufficient—just a T-shirt and shorts. Mom hurries me back to the lobby, where Mr. Kresge stands with arms raised behind the parapet that divides the lobby from the office, about to bring the metal divider down.

I'm closing up, he says, stretching for the divider's handle.

My mother's chin trembles.

Can't you wait, John? Please wait, John!

My God, he cries, his attention caught. What's wrong, Pauline?

My mother explains in hushed tones. He listens with his fingers on his mouth, his eyes growing ever wider; and then he thrusts the divider fully back so it retracts, clattering, into the ceiling. He sets the office phone on the counter. She lifts the receiver and pushes three buttons that I already know are 911.

Here we go, she says.

Mr. Kresge recedes into the dark office, then reappears a moment later with a yellow zip-hood sweatshirt with the school mascot, a cougar, screen-printed in blue on the back.

Yo, Zinnia.

I'm standing twisted because I only shaved one leg that day and I'm hoping he won't notice. He leans over the parapet, chucks me under the chin.

Hi, I squeak.

Hi, he squeaks back, mocking my awkwardness in a way that encourages me, makes me want to be bold. He hands me the sweatshirt.

Put this on. You must be freezing. Your legs are blue, he says.

Oh, shit. He noticed. Of course he did. I knew I should have shaved them both.

I shrug into the sweatshirt and zip it up. Behind me, my mother's voice grows more relaxed. She has reached a dispatcher.

Ah, Mr. Kresge says. Help is on the way.

He looks at me for a long moment.

What? I say.

My tone is disrespectful, but I don't have any other words. He smiles.

What, nothing. There's a quiz tomorrow. Don't forget.

I won't forget.

Attagirl, he says.

Mr. Kresge retreats behind the counter and begins to staple packets of mimeographs.

I slide to the floor, I smile and smile. My bones are nothing, puddle, mush. *Attagirl*, I tell myself. *Attagirl.*

My mother is dialing again, another number. Home,

I think. She's calling home. I hear my father shouting through the phone.

Of course we're at school, my mother snarls.

When they finish their conversation, she slams down the receiver and presses both hands against her eyes.

Mr. Kresge's eyebrows twitch with concern. You okay, Pauline?

Honestly, John. My husband could not be more delighted to hear about the car! It makes no sense. Sometimes I have no idea what goes through that man's head.

What goes through his head is Grand Theft Auto. Don't worry, Pauline! You'll get the insurance money *and* a brand-new car. Just wait and see. Think of the possibilities.

He is nodding in his teacherly way. He does just the same thing in class when we dissect frogs and earthworms and ask "well-formed" questions about whatever we've just extracted from their bodies. All questions are good questions, he says, but not all of them are *well formed.*

My mother grabs my backpack off the floor.

Since when do you sit *that way* in your short-shorts? Get up, she says. We're leaving.

Mr. Kresge says kindly: Have a good night, Pauline. As good as you can, anyway, under the circumstances.

The thing about Mr. Kresge is, the laugh is always in his voice, even when he's not laughing.

Outside, the police are already in the parking lot. My mother waves them over, and they take her statement. They tell her the car is probably in the hands of a joy-rider who sooner or later will run out of gas; the car will turn up eventually. My mother listens, gnawing at her fingernails.

My father arrives a few minutes later in the Mercury. For all the trouble, he seems strangely elated. He thumps the wheel. He cackles.

You've been subbing every day at the worst schools in the state and you get your car stolen from the fancy suburban school's parking lot! Who'da thunk, Pauline?

My mother flips the visor down and reapplies her lipstick in agitated strokes. I stay quiet. It is the prudent course, given the heat coming off both of them.

You don't seem too concerned about the theft, Stanley.

No, he says. I am not.

It's not your job on the line, I guess.

What she means is that without a car, she can't go to work. She gets her teaching assignments by phone at the last minute, with less than an hour before she has to appear at her assigned school, which could be anywhere in the city. Without a car, she'll be late every day.

The ride home is quiet. My father shifts the gears with a vicious exactness. On the highway, he floors it and leans back, loosening his grip on the wheel.

What's the matter with you, Pauline? We got plenty of money. You don't need to work. Or if you do, you can take the bus like everyone else.

Her laughter is short and brittle.

The bus? That's a nonstarter, and you know it.

This part of the road is long and straight. The world whips past, a blur. My mother stares at a point far ahead.

What's the matter, Pauline? You dreaming of the Big Banana?

It didn't have to be a fancy car, she says. Just something to get me from point A to point B.

You've missed my point.

I have not, she says. Unfortunately.

21

When Mom is furious, my father describes her using special words: *on the warpath, spoiling for a fight.*

I don't know about spoiling or the warpath, but I do know Mom has plenty of reasons to feel stressed. Without her car, she had to quit her job, and now Papa Frank's cancer has returned, and this time it's in his bones. Mom says when this happens, there's nothing anyone can do about it. He gets painkillers and oxygen, but that's about it. Still, she dresses up and drives him, using his car, to his doctor's appointments, and afterward they go to the donut shop.

It's a good day, my mother says, if she can persuade him to choke down a donut. He likes the Q-shaped kind called old-fashioned. They're as plain as you can get, and they taste of grease and sugar, and each has a little tail that Papa Frank likes to hold on to while dipping the rest in his coffee. He teases my mother, too, and tries to get her to break her diet, pointing out the French crullers, shiny with glaze, and the powdered donuts that ooze red jelly. After donuts, she takes him back to his house where Grandma Tina has installed an

oxygen tank in the living room along with his new hos-
pital-style bed, which she has cranked up so he can see
the view through the picture window. The view goes
right down to the water, to the huge wide cylinders of
fuel oil topped with little red lights like candles to keep
the planes away.

I wonder if he misses his old room, but I don't ask.
The view's better in his new situation, and it's easier
for Grandma Tina to look after him. For a long time
she has slept away from him, in the living room, and it
occurs to me only now to wonder at this arrangement,
which predates my arrival and which I already know
better than to ask about.

22

In Mr. Kresge's science class, we're doing a unit on space. We learn the names of all the planets in the solar system in order, from nearest to farthest from the sun. To help us remember them, he gives us a mnemonic: Mary's Violet Eyes Make John Sit Up Nights Pining.

His name is John, which gives me pause. Whose violet eyes have this effect on him? His own eyes are blue, often bloodshot, with very red rims.

Allergies, he says, wiping tears, when Donnie Murphy asks. His bold question has a mean edge, but Mr. Kresge is unfazed. He's seen kids like Donnie before, kids who smell like moldy clothes and keep knives in their socks just in case they need to cut someone, which I bet Donnie sometimes does. When the bell rings, he's almost always the first one out the door.

Allergies, Donnie scoffs. To teaching?

Good one, Donnie.

My mother says that allergies have nothing to do with it, that Mr. Kresge looks that way because he drinks. She says he drinks because he's lonely, and he's lonely because he wants a wife. She says these things with an intensity that makes me uncomfortable. For her or for myself, I can't tell.

I don't know what Mr. Kresge wants romantically, but I do think Donnie's right. Mr. Kresge does not enjoy teaching. Not always, anyway. Who *could* stand us, day after day?

Today Mr. Kresge punts the lesson and shows a filmstrip instead. An image of the solar system appears on the big white screen. It's late, and the classroom is dark apart from the light of the projector. Donnie slumps over his desk, his eyelids heavy.

What's this? Mr. Kresge asks.

The solar system, we chorus.

You kids sure know your lines.

The projector hums. The end-day bell will break the weird spell that has come over us. Meanwhile we're sitting in the dark attempting to get a better look at the sun.

I close my Trapper Keeper and hug it to my chest. This does not make the clock move faster. I distract myself with nonsense phrases, silently repeating *guinea canoe, three little guineas, sartor, restart us.*

Whoever Sartor is. I suppose we all pray to different gods.

Mr. Kresge, I say, without raising my hand. The classroom's darkness has made me bold.

What, Zinnia?

Could you buy a house out there? Set yourself up on Jupiter or one of its moons like those kids in the Madeleine L'Engle book, those kids in Camelot—

Camazotz, Mr. Kresge corrects me.

Donnie lifts his shaggy head: What the hell is Camazotz?

I'm pretty sure that's a well-formed question, but Mr. Kresge only says: *Language*.

I'm just asking, says Donnie. *Sheesh*.

No one owns the planets, Mr. Kresge says. Or anything on them. Why in the world, Zinnia—why would anyone want to buy a house on another planet?

The remark is gentle, not even teasing, but even so, I'm crushed. How stupid to ask about a thing like that.

Starter, restart us, I pray, waiting for the bell.

What about the moon, objects Donnie, raising his head.

What *about* the moon, Donnie?

The moon belongs to MTV, Donnie continues. They even put a flag on it.

The bell rings, and I beat Donnie to the door.

23

Over the summer I develop the habit of reading cheap novels while stretched on the sofa sucking down six-packs of Diet Coke. I keep this up even after school begins, lazing around on weekends and holidays, ignoring my schoolwork in favor of Danielle Steel and Stephen King and Sweet Valley High. Periodically my mother pads in, barefooted, to collect the empty cans. Today she's wearing an ivory teddy and seems unaware that the curtains are open. Her exhibitionism—I see this more clearly in retrospect—is evidence of her deepening distress, but at the time I can't find anything to fault. After all, I am nearly naked myself, wearing just a tank top and short-shorts. I tell myself the problem is the weather—the air conditioning isn't equal to the lingering summer heat.

She huffs and puffs, making a big theatrical deal of clearing my empties. She wants me to clean up after myself, but she also wants a tidy room. Her desire for the latter gives me the advantage, which I have lately begun to press and press. I'm getting a taste for it, this pressing. I like having power.

The shitty novels are also a problem. She'd probably prefer that I read *Sartor Restart Us* or *The Three Guineas*, but I'm not into economics and I'm absolutely tired of thinking about cars. I prefer stories like the one I'm reading, in which parents love their angelic children so much they do crazy things, like burying them in a magic cemetery—a *sematary*, is how the kids spell it, because they're kids—that brings them back to life as demons. Their parents are so glad to have them back, they don't even mind the changes.

I like these stories of angels and demons, the one turning into the other, diabolical.

Without a car, my mother can't go anywhere. Neither can I. These days Zenobia's the one who's always out. She has new friends now. *Fast* friends, my mother calls them, not totally disapprovingly. They don't know me or my slower, squarer friends and don't care to, and it is perhaps because of this that Zenobia launched herself so fully into their world. I sense that Mother would like me to do the same. She is not happy to have me lying around the house all day.

I crack the tab on another Diet Coke, holding it close to my face so my nostrils are prickled by the tiny burst of carbonated air.

My mother's standing half-naked at the window

again, sighing at the empty road and allowing the entire neighborhood to observe her in her teddy. *Oh, Maple Bay!* she cries theatrically as she pulls the curtains shut and returns to the reality of being home alone with me. She sighs hard as she sinks into the sofa, pushing my feet aside to make room.

Binkie Marfeo moved away, she says. Did you hear? They bought a faux Tudor monstrosity in Green Estates for a quarter million *bucks*.

Green Estates is where the ritzy people live. Guineas with guineas. I turn a page, glance down and up.

Faux Tudor? That's bad.

A crime, she replies, especially for that money. But what kills me is how she landed on her feet, smelling like a rose.

I ponder this, the feet that smell like roses, and wiggle my toes against her bare thigh, where the skin dimples. From the edge of her teddy her pubic hair peeks out, and I can't help noticing how dark it is, like mine, which is much darker than the hair on my head.

Stop it, she says. Look at you, ruining a library book. Don't dog-ear those pages, you'll have to pay for them.

It's not a library book.

Don't tell me you spent your own money on that garbage.

I found it in the dollar bin. It's getting all the respect it deserves.

Your logic is unassailable, Zinnia. But your discernment leaves a lot to be desired.

Relenting, I change the subject: Binkie might not be so lucky in her new digs, you know.

What do you mean?

Think about it. After our car was stolen, Binkie became the only one in the neighborhood with a guinea canoe. Who knows what crimes might befall her now, in Green Estates, and how she might find herself elevated?

I speak grandly, like a television announcer, to make my mother laugh. She does, which is gratifying, but then she leans across the sofa and tugs at my crop top: I don't understand why you can't dress like a normal child.

I'm not a child!

Not a normal one, you mean.

Her friendly teasing makes me feel better—about her, the summer, Zenobia's new friends, all of it. She's doing better, I think. She even smells more like herself—cold cream and Chanel No. 5. I'm glad for this, and I don't mind it, but for myself I like a different perfume.

Now, don't pout.

I'm not pouting, I say, though I *am* pouting, a little. A lecture's in the offing, but for once, I don't really mind. It dawns on me that this is why her pothos grows and grows. It feels attended to.

You can't go around all hussy, Zinnia.

Says you, waltzing around in a teddy with the curtains open.

I'm a grown woman. I do what I want.

Why can't I then?

You know why not. You'll get a *rep*.

She says *rep* with a weird gusto. She means a *reputation*, whatever that meant in her own school days, but she also makes it sound as if a *rep* were some exciting cause for admiration, like having a wild boyfriend or fast friends with cars. *Rep* is the sound of jeans ripping, of buttons popping; it's the sound of the unsupervised time between school and dinner. *Rrrepp*.

The boys will think you're *damaged goods*, she continues.

That reminds me, I say. There's a sale at the department store.

Very funny, Zinnia. So why don't you go? Get some air.

Get out of your hair, you mean.

That too.

I suppose I might as well go. I need another bottle of *L'Air du Temps*.

Oh, *L'Air du Temps*. Your favorite.

Do you know what it means, Mom? *L'air du temps?*

My schoolgirl French is too rusty even to hazard a guess. What do you think it means?

Our eyes meet. She's smiling. What *does* it mean, this odd French phrase?

Well, I say, *l'air* could just be what you breathe. It's also something you put on, like an attitude. Which makes it nice as a name for a perfume. But an air is also a kind of song. So maybe it means *song of time*.

She looks at me. Don't move, she says.

She leaves and comes back waving a green clutch of bills which she pushes into my palm.

My treat, she says.

It's ten dollars—almost half her allowance for the week. While I'm counting she slips out of the room. She's gone before I can thank her.

I fold the bills up small and tuck the bundle into my pocket where it makes a little lump. I'm saving it for later because this book I'm reading, cheap as it is, is also very hard to put down. In the story, all the pets are coming back from the dead. Dogs, cats, guinea pigs, hamsters—it's incredible. Then a child toddles in front of a semi and the truck can't stop and neither can I.

When I finally finish the book, it's like someone

hit me in the face. When you bury something in the *sematary*, it doesn't come back as a demon. It comes back as *damaged goods*.

It's too late for shopping, and I'm no longer in the mood. What I want is to be with my dog, the one who is not yet in any sematary or cemetery, but whose mortality increasingly preoccupies me. Bixby can't run outside anymore because his legs are going. His ears are still silky, but the edges are ragged, and his muzzle is almost completely white. He spends most of his time asleep on the cushion by the heater.

Bixby's appetite is as strong as ever, though, and I feed him everything I can get my hands on. Today it's a can of macaroni and cheese—in those days, you could get it in a can—and even though he can hardly walk he licks my fingers clean. When he's done eating I bury my nose in the soft spot at the top of his head, breathing in his gamy smell.

You won't die, I tell him as he nuzzles my palm, searching for one last loop of noodle.

But if he did, I would definitely bury him in the pet sematary.

I don't care if you're a demon, I say. I would always want you back.

24

Against doctor's orders and all good sense, Papa Frank is smoking again. He's done with life, he says. He only smokes, though, when it's just me and him alone together at his house. Camels, unfiltered, the kind he likes. At this point no one has the heart to stop him. No one worries about the oxygen either, so when we're together I make sure to turn the canister's knob to the OFF position.

Might as well, he says as he lights up. You only live once—and once is enough!

Mom says he's not tired of living, just tired of being sick. She doesn't like his smoking. She wants him to live a long time, longer than he thinks he's likely to. He's coughing a lot now, much more than before. When we watch television in the living room, he spits up orange phlegm into an old plastic juice container. It's always full.

Get up and change the channel, he tells me. I'm tired of this ballgame.

I thought you were tired of life.

That too. Go on, get up. It's a rerun anyway. I saw the game once already and that's enough for anyone.

Like life? I ask, standing.

He says: Exactly.

I flip the dial until he stops me at an old episode of *Looney Tunes*. His favorite character is Yosemite Sam. Mine is the Tasmanian Devil. I like his huge mouth and his white teeth and the way he shamelessly bites through everything—pine trees, chain mail, leather shoes.

That one can really eat, Papa Frank says. Wish I felt the same, to be honest.

Over the next few months he gets worse and worse. Eventually he's not even able to get out of bed. The picture window leaks, so now, when I'm with him, I tuck him up with an extra blanket of heavy wool, cobalt blue. We watch *The Lawrence Welk Show* and *Fantasy Island*, *Hollywood Squares* and *Family Feud*.

At the bottom of the dark hillside, lights are strung along the port like an icy diamond necklace, the sort I'd never wear but that I'd like to give, someday, to my mother. But right now I'm not doing anything with diamonds or necklaces. I'm just here with Papa Frank and the oxygen. I hold his hand. He's lost so much weight he's almost nothing at this point, just loose skin and his long old bones, his exposed forearm a pale slash against the blanket. A tear rolls down my face.

Don't cry, he whispers. Please don't cry.

25

The phone rings one night in January. It's so bitter cold, I am sleeping in trash bags because they retain my body's heat better than my blankets.

Tina, calm down, my father is saying. Tina, I don't understand. I can't understand you unless you calm down.

There is a pause, and then my mother is talking, her voice pitched so high and tight the back of my neck prickles. A shadow crosses the room; something that normally lives inside me is on the outside now, loose.

I press my ear to the wall. My teeth chatter: Bitter-cold.

The phone slams into the cradle. My mother cries: We have to go to the hospital!

Ah ha, my father laughs. Ah ha ha ha!

Stanley—

A-a-a-n-d and how will you get there, Pauline?

26

My mother deteriorates. That's the only word I have to describe what happens. She loses weight. She doesn't sleep. She paints a portrait of Jesus in a sky-blue coat with his back turned to the viewer.

That's just how I felt when he died, she says. Like Jesus had turned his back on me.

Every day while my sister and I are in school she takes the bus to the Salvation Army where she buys old-fashioned dresses in ragged sateen and yellowed lace. She wears them accessorized with large garish earrings made of dozens of black faceted plastic beads, not my father's. He calls these earrings "funeral house chandeliers." In her wacky getups she becomes embarrassing. I can't stand to have her pick me up from school, which she insists on doing even though that means she must borrow my father's car. Everyone gives her weird looks. Mr. Kresge turns to me and whispers, *Your mother's none too tightly wrapped, is she?*

Later I will replay the phrase to myself, find excuses to use it in conversation with my friends. *This ice cream sandwich is none too tightly wrapped. Your salami hoagie is none too tightly wrapped.* For some reason, it's the funniest thing I've heard.

Maybe it's the reproductive angle. Lately my friends have been telling wild stories about high school; there's a rumor that in health class, the teacher demonstrates using condoms by stretching them over cucumbers and bananas. It's enough to send anyone into a fit of hysterics and that's how most of my classes end, with everyone beet-red and gasping about things that are or are not *tightly wrapped*. I know I shouldn't join in, but I can't help myself. My mother's going crazy, my grandfather is dead, and to top it all, so is Bixby. I'm taking laughs wherever I can get them.

When Bixby died, my father slid his body into a trash bag, slung the parcel over his shoulder, and went out in the rain to dig. He set the parcel on the lawn at the far edge of the yard and crouched down, passing his hand over his face. I think he was sobbing. Then he stood, a dark figure hoisting a shovel, alone with our dead dog and the task of burying him.

I was watching from the window, my mother's overgrown plant tickling my ears. My mother padded up behind me and peered over my shoulder.

The changing of the guard, she sighed.

I heard a snip. I turned to see her leaving with a long tail of leaves held in one hand. Why trim the plant tonight of all nights? Another mystery. I felt ashamed, as if she had snipped the plant as a criticism, a way of snipping me. Outside my father was setting the bag in the hole he'd dug. The bag was not large; in fact it was small, forlorn, as if Bixby had been dying by degrees for a long time. Maybe he had been, and I just didn't notice. Or I couldn't allow myself to see. Once, near the end, a maggot squirmed out of the pad of his paw. He must have been in pain, yet I turned away, told no one. Did nothing. Now I couldn't put the image out of my mind. I still can't.

In my room I wedged myself beneath the gap between my bed and the cold wall. I pressed my ear to it and listened. My body's roar was distant, but it was there. Outside, the noise of the shovel, my father at his sad work.

That night Mom painted another self-portrait, this time of herself in her ivory teddy, perched on the edge of the bed she shared with my father and holding a pale-yellow rose. Her eyes were huge, like cartoon eyes, and the charcoal under-drawing was still visible, coming through the dashed-on paint.

27

A few days before the trial begins, JT fails to show up for work. His absence stretches over days, then weeks. My father falls into his familiar black funk. But this time when he slams all the doors, I don't startle. As the house reverberates, something inside me goes to ground, like a rabbit shadowed suddenly by a hawk. My heart beats a little slower, and a little slower still. These days I hardly ever leave my room. My closet has depths that cry out for exploring. I still fit, barely, into the space beneath the bed.

Sunk deep in his personal darkness, my father unloads more often on my mother, launching himself into tirades that only make sense to him. Tonight, while he rants, my mother flips the steak she's frying, sets down the pan, and removes one huge jangling earring and then the other, setting them in a saucer she keeps in the kitchen for this purpose. She is feeling better, but she's still wearing the ancient dresses, the terrible earrings.

Time to face reality, Stanley. The bird has flown the coop.

She looks as if she would like to do the same. The funeral house chandeliers glint in their saucer.

He didn't even collect his check, Pauline! You'd think a guy like that would at least collect his check.

Oh, a guy *like that*. Like what, I ask you. Besides, what do you care if he doesn't collect his check? It just means more for you.

My father, who must surely have understood the role he'd played in the cover-up that followed the killing, puts his head in his hands.

28

My father gets a call. Lo and behold, a car corresponding to the description of my mother's Lincoln has been found, dumped somewhere in the western part of the state. Now my father has to go down to the police station to pick it up.

Do they know who took it? my mother asks.

Joyriders is what the police figure. Some kids took the car for a spin and left it wherever they ran out of gas.

My mother frowns. That's what they said when it was stolen.

Looks like they weren't wrong! my father cries. I have no idea why he is so giddy.

Does this mean we have to return the insurance money?

My father: Oh, Pauline, you don't need to worry your pretty head about that.

29

The next day, my father returns home with the Lincoln. I'm in the kitchen when he arrives, rinsing dishes before stacking them inside the dishwasher. He honks as he pulls into the driveway, and I run to the door. Racing up behind me, Zenobia arrives just as I do. She elbows past, breathing: *Me first.*

Her breath stinks of her fast friends' cigarettes, and there's scum on her teeth because she hates to brush them. *Me first, me first, me first.*

My father gets out and stalks around our Lazarus car, touching the ragtop, the paint job.

Unbelievable. Pauline. Will you get a load of this!

It's a lot to take in. Large decals of Playboy bunnies now adorn the mud flaps, and the door locks are framed by smaller bunnies cut like cookies from flattened chrome. Inside, the cassette player has been messily yanked out and replaced with an old 8-track. It doesn't quite fit and in the gaps between the 8-track and its receptacle I see loose wires hanging. Other things are also different. Where there was fancy marled wood, there is now only cheap metal, and the plush velour is not so plush either. It's as if my mother has magicked one of her *skinny substitutions*, presto change-o, on the whole car.

My father wants to take this weird car for a spin. Wants my mother to drive. He talks fast, pushing us toward the car, opening the doors wide. Obediently we pile in.

My mother starts the engine. But the shift doesn't want to shift. She pushes and tugs, putting her whole upper body into it: Jesus, that's stiff!

My father: I'll bet it was, Pauline!

What the hell is that supposed to mean?

I just hope you got your money's worth, is all.

Very funny, she says. Everyone's a comedian these days.

When she turns out the corner, she has to rotate the wheel in great movements, like a trucker. She says: Something's not right. The power steering's out of commission.

So? Ask the mechanic to look into it.

This doesn't feel like the same car. Are you sure it's the same car?

The VIN numbers match. Why else do you think they called *us*? You're an intelligent woman, Pauline.

Don't tell me you can't figure out how this works—

All right, all right, Stanley—

You with your fancy Connecticut people, and all your fancy education, your *master's* degree—

I said all right, Stanley!

All I'm saying is, if there's some other VIN number, that's someone else's car.

My mother's face is white.

Forget it, she says. I'll manage.

When Mom parks in the driveway, she struggles again with shift, pulling and yanking until the rod moves. Her jaw is set, but she's shaking. Freddy's truck is parked in the driveway, too, and there's banging— Freddy's going at the roof with his hammer.

Well, look who's back from the dead, my father murmurs.

Crabwise Freddy makes his way across the roof and down the ladder. He ambles over to shake my father's hand: Nice to see ya, Stanley.

My mother says, waveringly: They found the car.

Freddy takes one look at it—the mud flaps, the keyholes—and hoots.

Pauline, he gasps. Oh, Pauline.

What can I do, she implores him—me, us. *What can I actually do?*

30

It has taken many years, but at last I see the wisdom of my mother's *skinny substitutions*. Her whole life was one big *skinny substitution*, a front that was as false and dull as it was necessary. Behind it, one might live. Take a breath or two. At night, drive your husband's expensive car past the seacoast house of another man.

The change, at first, is so subtle, it's easy to pretend it's nothing at all. My mother takes us for one of her rides. My sister and I shut ourselves into the car's maroon interior, pretending that everything's normal, that this car really *is* the same one that we lost. It's as if the harder we try, the easier it will be to ignore the strange additions and deletions—the Playboy keyholes, the 8-track player, the weird velour. My mother is still struggling with the gearshift.

We take the usual route. I continue to squint my feelings, tightening my focus so all the troubling details disappear and I can almost believe we're back in the old days, when JT was still running the factory and Mr. Marfeo was still alive. And so was my dog. And Papa Frank.

Actually, I'm not so sure he's dead. I'm not sure about Bixby, either. Maybe they're both still out there, somewhere—like in *Pet Sematary*, but less diabolical. Friendlier. After all that's happened, I have learned something. The changing of a guard is not the decimation of it.

But, point of fact: Mr. Marfeo is definitely dead. JT would not have gone to jail otherwise. And Binkie would not have her Tudor monstrosity in Green Estates. Some truths you can tell by their consequences.

In the back seat my sister has her nose stuck deep in yet another Sweet Valley High. In this one, the twins switch identities. The smart one skips town while the dumb one stays home and pretends to be the smart one. That's who the story is about, she who stays home and pretends.

What happens to the other one? The one who leaves?

Zenobia looks up.

Who cares? she asks.

Maybe she goes to Canberra, I say.

Why Canberra? my mother asks.

She wants to try the veggie mites?

Vegemite, she corrects me. Australians spread it on their toast.

Have *you* tried it?

She snaps: When would I have ever tried Vegemite?

Her life, she means, has not included this possibility. Vegemite is not available in the grocery stores of Maple Bay.

Maybe she goes to the moon, Zenobia says.

Oh, the *moon,* my mother scoffs. What a stupid ruse. The whole thing is stupid. I can't understand why you read those books, Zenobia.

Me neither, I say, agreeing with my mother. It is the best of developments, a chance to make the playing field two against one, or really one against one: the smarty-pants mother-daughter unit against she who stays home and pretends.

Shut up, my sister says. Just shut the fuck up, Zinnia.

My mother murmurs, *Language.*

We're on the highway, picking up speed. I stretch myself across the maroon cushions, which are not as cushiony as they were before. Night is coming on, starrier and starrier. There's a big pink moon. If it's a ruse, it's a pretty one.

Zenobia has been grouchy ever since Papa Frank died. My mother says she's depressed. She cries all the time. My mother says she can adopt a cat. Maybe that will cheer her up, she says.

I miss my dog and I miss Papa Frank. I used to cry, but then my mother caught me crying and screamed at me: *What are you crying about? You didn't lose YOUR father.* I stopped crying after that. I stopped feeling much of anything. Now the only time I feel anything is when I'm being mean to Zenobia. Being mean to Zenobia makes me feel amazing. It fills me with icy joy.

Why can't I get a cat too, Mom?

Zinnia, don't push.

Am I pushing? I am probably pushing. What's different is that Mom's objection now feels empty, *pro forma*. When I'm mean to Zenobia, it's the same thing. No one seems to care. I can act with impunity. Maybe.

I kick off my sneakers and throw my legs over the front seat. My left leg brushes against my mother's bare arm. She frowns: You're still pushing, Zinnia.

Wanting attention feels like wanting candy: you don't exactly need it, but you'll do stupid things to get it.

Maah—om, I singsong. *Mom.*

She pushes my leg away. Stop it, Zinnia.

In my best movie-star voice: This velour's simply all wrong, *Muhtherrr.*

Zinnia, didn't anyone ever tell you that you need to shave the *backs* of your legs too?

Mom, the *velour*. The vel-ooh-ah.

The velour. For God's sake, Zinnia—you and *the ve-lour.* What about it?

It's not the same as before the car was stolen.

The road goes *whoosh.* The night goes *whoosh.* Something in my mind goes *whoosh.*

It's not the same car.

Oh, the icy joy that floods my veins.

It's so dark out here, and yet I am seeing with complete clarity: I am in the middle. When my sister is around, I am in the middle. The problem with being in the middle is that those on either side would like to get rid of you. Two's company. Three is something else, beyond my mother's ability to cope.

An insight can compensate for so much grief, I say.

What insight, my mother says.

It's not really a question. Her attention's caught on something else.

We're at the railroad crossing. Mom lets the car roll up, too close. The lights flash as the long bar comes down.

I have so completely underestimated Sweet Valley High, I say.

The train approaches, distant lights closing in.

One crime may hide another, my mother says, glancing over her shoulder. She struggles with the shift, trying to get the car into reverse. One train, one car, one girl—

Mom—

The gears catch, and we spurt backward, out of harm's way.

Voilà, says my mother. *WAH-LAH!*

My heart's pounding, but there was never any real danger. It's just a slow-going freight train, and it hoots as it passes by, courteous: The conductor sees us and wants us to know. My mother replies by flashing the headlights. It's a nice moment. Sane.

Then we are heading toward the turn to the old road, familiar as a phrase that plays between stations and suggests a whole song. In front of Mr. Kresge's house, the street is empty, swept free of everything that might disturb the evening's peace. The condominiums are small but neat and bright. As the wind picks up, the pretty lanterns swing brightly in the entryways.

Mom flicks the headlights, saying: Look at the house divorce built.

My crush on Mr. K. has ebbed, but my mother seems not to have gotten the memo.

Whose divorce? Zenobia asks.

Never mind.

Mr. Marfeo is also no longer a central matter of

concern. My family is—my parents, specifically. This will be true for the rest of my life. What's happened has hollowed me out, so I'm just a tube the wind blows through. Memory, also—like a wind.

What if Mr. Kresge sees you, Mom?

She snorts. Me? Why would *he* see *me*?

The ride gets quiet. I remember something someone—was it Freddy?—once said to my mother: *A man makes a world around himself.*

And everyone else has to find a way to live in it, she had replied.

I stare at the dashboard controls, mesmerized, until Zenobia whacks me, hard, with Sweet Valley High.

Bitch! I shout.

I reach into the front seat and grab around wildly, aiming for anything, until I come up with a handful of Zenobia's hair. I yank, hard, and she howls as she throws the book at me. I catch it with my free hand, the one not tangled in her hair, and a plan forms in my mind.

I hit the switch, and the moonroof glides open. A moment later, Sweet Valley High is in the rearview, bouncing on the shoulder.

That was a library book!

No, it wasn't.

Yes, it was.

I slip to the floor, run my hands over the carpet. Pushing my fingers through the pile I sense pressure. A thick strand of white hair wraps itself around the knuckles of one hand.

Through the roof, the sky grows heavy. Clouds are moving in. A streetlight comes on as we pass beneath it, and then we're swinging away, out of Mr. Kresge's subdivision. We reach the highway and my mother revs the engine, coaxing the car up to speed.

I lift my hands up through the open roof, letting the wind take them, take everything, the fluff from the carpet, the twisted white strand of hair.

L'air du temps, my mother says sadly. *The song of time.*

There's a whistling emptiness in my chest, space for everything my father felt free to do to her, everything they felt free to do to each other.

If I'm going to get out, I need to get beyond this.

Point of fact: I have no idea how to get beyond this.

Wind rushes into our red chamber. The moon silvers me through the gap.

What a time to be alive, my mother says. A little night music, my lovelies?

Without waiting for an answer, my mother turns on the radio and spins the knob until she catches a song we know. We sing along, shouting through the opening as if no one can hear us. We're right: No one can.